TINYRANNOSAURUS
AND THE
NEVERSAURUS

By
Nick Ward

meadowside

Tinyrannosaurus (wrecks) loves his bedtime stories, and because he is the fiercest little dinosaur ever, he especially likes **SCARY** stories.

The scarier the better!

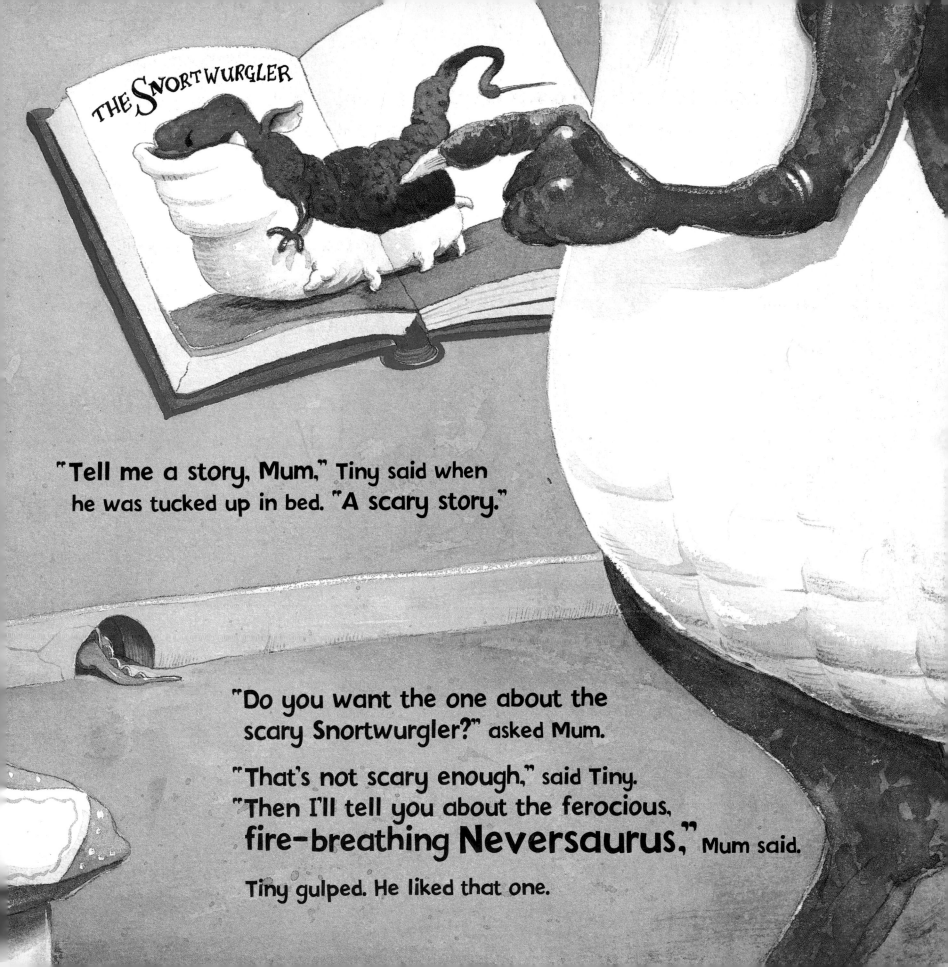

THE SNORTWURGLER

"Tell me a story, Mum," Tiny said when he was tucked up in bed. "A scary story."

"Do you want the one about the scary Snortwurgler?" asked Mum.

"That's not scary enough," said Tiny.
"Then I'll tell you about the ferocious,
fire-breathing **Neversaurus**," Mum said.

Tiny gulped. He liked that one.

"When the moon is high and the night is dark, the ferocious, fire-breathing Neversaurus pads quietly through the streets," said Mum.

"Gnashing his big yellow teeth, the Neversaurus peers through the windows and growls through the locks, making sure all little dinosaurs are safely tucked up in bed...

"Even though no one has ever
seen the Neversaurus, you must
be very careful, because if the
Neversaurus ever sees a little
dinosaur like you out
after dark, he..."

But there Mum stopped,
because Tinyrannosaurus
was already fast asleep!

Early the next morning, Tiny made some sandwiches, got out his biggest fishing net and marched into the garden. "Where are you going?" asked Mum.

"I'm going to catch that ferocious, fire-breathing **Neversaurus**," said Tiny.

"Well, make sure you are back in time for tea," smiled Mum.

Tinyrannosaurus wasn't scared of anything and he roared his loudest roar as he tiptoed through the jewel bright jungle, fishing net at the ready.

"This is just the sort of place to find a Neversaurus," he thought.

And then, he heard a noise coming from the undergrowth. A rumbling, wheezing noise.

"I'll help," said Baby Kong,
and they roared their loudest roars
and pulled their fiercest faces
and went on their way.

"This is just the sort of place to find a Neversaurus," whispered Tiny as they tiptoed up to the edge of the bubbling, sulphurous swamp.

"There he is," said Baby Kong, pointing to a large horn sticking out of the mud.

FLOP!

Tiny swung his net. "Got you, you horrible Neversaurus!" they bellowed.

"I'll help," said Dinoceros, and they roared
their loudest roars and crashed their mighty jaws
and went off to find the ferocious,
fire-breathing **Neversaurus.**

"We are bound to find the Neversaurus here," said Tiny, after they had waded through the tall, prickly prairie grass and climbed to the top of a boulder.

They looked all around. "There he is," cried Dinoceros. Tiny swung his net.

"Oh no! This is ridiculous," yelled Tiny, getting very grumpy indeed. All they had caught was a rather dozy Brontosaurus, munching lazily on the grass. **"We'll never find the Neversaurus at this rate."**

"Let's climb the big volcano," suggested Baby Kong. **"We'll be able to see for miles and miles from there."**

So the three friends marched off to the big volcano.

The sun started to set as they looked
out over the valley. They couldn't see
a Neversaurus anywhere.

"Perhaps we should go home," shivered Baby Kong.
"If the Neversaurus finds us out after dark, he'll..."

"I'm not scared of him," said Tinyrannosaurus.
"We've looked everywhere.
I DON'T BELIEVE THERE IS
SUCH A THING AS A SILLY
NEVERSAURUS,"
he shouted.

But if only they could see what you can see!

The ferocious Neversaurus roared his mightiest roar, blowing plumes of smoke and coils of fire into the air.

"Quick," cried the friends, "The volcano is erupting!" And as the ground shook and the sky filled with flares and flashes and whizz-bangs, they scampered all the way down the hill.

"Good," smiled the Neversaurus. "They should get home in time for tea."

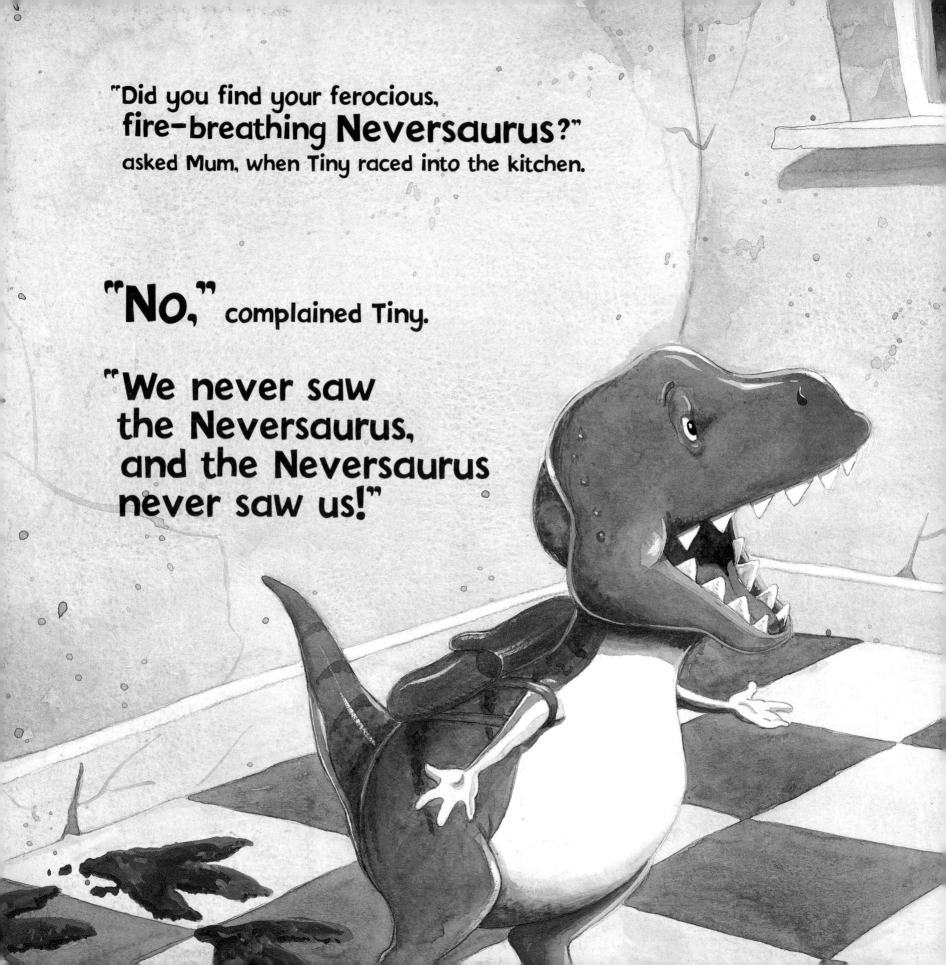

"Did you find your ferocious, **fire-breathing Neversaurus?**" asked Mum, when Tiny raced into the kitchen.

"**NO,**" complained Tiny.

"**We never saw the Neversaurus, and the Neversaurus never saw us!**"

For the very scary,
Mighty Markmilloseros.
Good hunting!

N.W.

First published in 2006
by Meadowside Children's Books
185 Fleet Street, London, EC4A 2HS
Text and illustrations © Nick Ward 2006

The right of Nick Ward to be
identified as the
author and illustrator of this
work has been
asserted by him in accordance
with the Copyright,
Designs and Patents Act, 1988

A CIP catalogue record for this book
is available from the British Library
Printed in China

ISBN 10 (PBK) 1-84539-193-4 · ISBN 13 (PBK) 978-1-84539-193-5
ISBN 10 (HBK) 1-84539-194-2 · ISBN 13 (HBK) 978-1-84539-194-2

10 9 8 7 6 5 4 3 2 1